# Destination Escape

### Learning to Love Again
### Book 1

## Rochelle Bradley

# DEDICATION


For Stephanie Johnson at Star City Booksellers. Thank you for creating a warm and welcoming environment for indie authors.
I appreciate you.

# ACKNOWLEDGMENTS

Thank you to Sara Cunningham for working with me to create the beautiful cover.
To Rebecca Aksdal for helping to perfect ***Destination Escape***.

To my Coffee Hub writing group… thank you for listening to me plot out loud, offering suggestions, and for all the laughs. I appreciate you helping to keep me focused.

# A NOTE FROM ROCHELLE

Dear Reader,

Thank you for grabbing book one in the Learning to Love Again series. It all started with a dream I had with Vanessa and her evil twin, Veronica.

I wrote ***The 24 Hour Bet*** first, but was so compelled with Vanessa's plight and her escape that I had to expand on it. After ***Destination Escape,*** you can continue to root for Vanessa to find her happily ever after in book 2 of the series.

Welcome to the world of the Warsaw and Tanner families.

Thanks again, and happy reading!

~Rochelle

# CHAPTER ONE

THE BLACK DRESS ACCENTED MY curves, and I felt like a million bucks. I counted on that boost of confidence to get me through the night. As I glanced around the restaurant lobby searching for my father, he caught my gaze and smiled. Cool and confident in his dark suit jacket, starched white shirt, and emerald green tie, he appeared ready to broker the deal of the century.

I loved my father, but I hated these dinners. Not the father-daughter meals, of course, but the ones where my father has invited some guy he wants to marry me off to. My father wanted to sell more than Warsaw Industries.

*The Warsaw Curse.*

I sighed. My inner voice was right.

Next to Dad was a tall, slender man, who I could only assume was the man du jour. I inhaled deeply and plastered on a fake smile. The young man reminded me of a gamer in a business suit: kinda cute but nerdy. Floppy, almost-too-long curls bounced as he tilted his head, sizing me up.

*Not hard on the eyes.*

"Who is he this time? The Senior Project Engineer over the U.S., or maybe the Purchasing Agent for our European division," I muttered, under my breath.

*Remember that IT Specialist? He had nice buns.*

And Roni had noticed them, too. I tried to shake off the negative memories and greeted my father. "Daddy."

"Hey babydoll," he acknowledged, taking my hands in his. He leaned in and kissed my cheek. Then he met my eyes. His brow crinkled as he inspected me. "You look tired. Maybe it's time for a vacation."

*You think? Little does he know…*

I swallowed. "Sounds like a great idea. I'll have Darlene check my schedule."

He squeezed my hands and nodded. "I brought a friend—"

"Here we go again." I rolled my eyes.

"Now Vanessa, it's not like that." He dropped my hands as the hostess invited us to follow her.

"Isn't it?" I hissed and brushed past him to follow the woman without giving the bewildered men a second thought.

*You go, girl.*

The hostess stopped at a round table covered with a burgundy cloth. The man pulled out a chair for me, and I thanked him as I sat. My father picked a seat next to me, while the stranger opted for the seat across from me, for which I gave silent thanks. I'd rather stare him in the eye than bump elbows.

*That's right. You aren't Roni.*

"Let me introduce you… Kyle, this is my beautiful daughter, Vanessa Warsaw. Vanessa, meet Kyle Davis."

I extended my arm across the table, and Kyle stood and took my hand, shaking it. He had a firm grip but didn't hold on too long. "It's a pleasure." His voice was high as if he had snuffed helium before speaking.

*What the what?*

"So, Kyle… which division do you work for?" I asked, holding his gaze and biting back a grin.

He reseated himself. "Please?"

My father and I shared a look. "Where do you work in our company?" I tried again.

Kyle's eyes widened, but before he could speak, Dad chuckled then clarified, "Kyle is the son of Richard, my golfing buddy."

"Oh, okay," I stammered. Kudos to Vic Warsaw shopping outside the company for potential husbands.

*When in war, you switch tactics to throw the enemy off.*

We ordered and, as I sipped my wine, I listened more than I spoke. The topic turned to the economy and Father made an offhand comment about an acquisition for our European division.

"Yeah, Dad told me about that," Kyle said. "Congratulations." He raised his glass.

My gaze narrowed. While not necessarily a national secret, our business deals weren't interesting enough to appear in the daily news or on social media sites. How had Kyle Davis' father known about it and why did he pass the knowledge on? Richard and Dad are golfing buddies sure, but would Dad go into the details on the course?

*Not when he could complain about the fairway, his swing, or the weather.*

Richard Davis. The name sounded familiar. I drummed my fingers on the table. At a lull in the conversation, while the men sampled their food, I asked, "What do you do for a living, Kyle?"

He dabbed his lips with the cloth napkin then smiled. In his chipmunk voice, he replied, "I'm a yoga instructor."

I froze, fork in front of my face. "Really?"

"No. But I do own a business where you can take yoga. We have a full gym and also offer classes, plus we have a nutritionist to help with meal plans." His gaze shifted to my father. "I enjoy the work. Love what I do."

"And your father?" I asked, certain I knew the name.

"He's a real estate attorney," Kyle squeaked.

*Get him to recite the preamble or something from Shakespeare.*

I contained my snort of laughter, covering it with a cough. Then it hit me where I knew the name Richard Davis—the shareholder listing. My gaze swung to my father and narrowed.

"I don't need you to play matchmaker, Father." I growled out the final word in a low tone.

*Probably three octaves lower than Kyle's.*

"Vanessa." My father used his we-will-talk-about-it-later voice.

I seethed. Inhaling through my nose, I exhaled through my mouth. My attention turned to Kyle. "I don't know on what pretense you were invited to dinner, but I'm not looking to get married." I rose, wadding my napkin.

"Vanessa, sit down." Father's face had morphed into an emotionless mask. "Please?"

I returned to the seat but crossed my arms.

*Time for the Ice Queen to take a stand.*

"Your 'golfing buddy' is one of our shareholders. I knew this was a setup. It aways is. Do you really want me to just settle for some average Joe—" I faced Kyle, "no offense." Turning my attention back to my father, I continued, "I will not settle for someone I don't love and a marriage that won't last, just to save the business from Grandma's stupid curse." As I spoke, my volume had increased. Several people studied our table.

"What curse?" Kyle asked, glancing from me to my father.

"Thank's to Grandma Warsaw, I must marry in order to keep the business in the family."

Dad leaned toward me. "We will talk it over later," he hissed.

I pressed against the stiff chair back. My lip curled into a sneer. "I am not a piece of meat you can toss to any single man. If you want me to be happy and actually give you grandkids, then let me find a partner for myself." When he opened his mouth, I jabbed the air with a finger. "There are less than three months until my birthday. I doubt I'll find, date, and marry a man in that time. And yes, I know it happened to you and Mom…" My breath hitched at mentioning my mother, and dad blanched as if I'd hit him. After all these years, her loss still stung.

I squeezed my eyes shut and refocused. When I opened them, Dad tapped the stem of his martini glass and Kyle worked on sawing his steak.

"Listen Dad, I know you want to save Warsaw Industries and keep it in the family, but I don't want to get married just for the hell of it."

"Don't you care what will happen to our employees?" he asked, his gaze hard.

"Don't you want me to be happy and find a relationship like you and Mom had?"

His cheeks flared red with anger… or shame. I couldn't tell. His mustache twitched. "You could learn to love—"

"What about Roni?" I tossed out. "Give Kyle to her because I'm not interested."

Kyle set his fork aside. "Who's Roni?"

I glanced at my watch. "You'll see. She'll be here any moment. She's my sister, and she has a habit of showing up to Daddy's matchmaking attempts. By the way, if you want to get lucky, just pretend to be interested in me. She'll spread her legs faster than the government racks up debt."

"Vanessa," Father snapped.

I shrugged and started a mental list of the items I needed to pack.

"There you are," Roni's voice floated over the restaurant din. She strutted to the table. Her red skirt exposed most of her thighs. The lace of her pushup bra peeked from her V-neck blouse. She leaned forward, giving Kyle a cleavage shot. "Who's this gorgeous creature?"

*Just another dick for you to ride.*

Kyle glanced at me, and I shrugged again. "You can have him," I told my sister.

"Vanessa," father snipped again, slowly shaking his head.

Roni took the seat between Kyle and me. She leaned toward him, probably rubbing her knee against his.

"Vanessa, what's it like to be the head of your family's business?" Kyle asked.

I chuckled, watching Roni squirm. Kyle must want to get laid. "Do you really want to know, or are you taking my advice?"

His cheeks blossomed pink. "I'd like to know."

Since he owned a business, he understood the ups and downs of the market. So, I launched into a speech I'd concocted for father's matchmaking schemes. One designed to stifle Roni's allure by boring her to death.

# CHAPTER TWO

*No going back now.*

I leaned away from the laptop screen and exhaled. This plane ticket had been the last thing I needed to escape the family curse.

Darlene cleared her throat. "Ms. Warsaw?" She hesitated between rooms.

Glancing at the door to my temporary office, I wondered how long she'd stood there. "Yes. What can I do for you, Dar?" I hurriedly closed the internet browser. I'd clear my history later.

She smiled and stepped forward, tablet in hand. "Are you all right?" She stopped in front of the desk, inspecting me over her fuchsia framed glasses.

I waved a hand. "Just tired. My mind had wandered to an upcoming retreat."

Darlene's brows rose, and her lips quirked to the side in a tic. "Oh?"

"I scheduled a massage." I rubbed my temples, then rolled my shoulders. No sense acknowledging my appointment would be fulfilled in another hemisphere.

"After what you've been through…" she sighed, not adding details. "You deserve it and more."

I appreciated her tact. She'd made a great administrative assistant and almost qualified as a friend. "Thank you."

"Back to business," Darlene said, waking her tablet.

"Must we," I mumbled.

She chuckled while tapping the screen. "Unfortunately, your father is insistent you look over the proposal he sent you."

I spun the desk chair so Darlene wouldn't see me roll my eyes and then stood and walked to the room's floor-to-ceiling window. The gray sky with churning clouds echoed my mood. The view from my office was ten times better, but I hadn't been able to stomach being there, let alone sitting at the desk where…

Darlene cleared her throat again, pulling me back from the misery.

"Don't we pay people to do that?" Facing Darlene, I crossed my arms.

"Of course, Ms. Warsaw, but you know your father."

I did indeed. "No rest for the weary." I sighed and reclaimed the plush leather chair. Although not mine, I'd found it comfortable.

Darlene hesitated, biting her lip. She tapped the

stylus on the side of the tablet.

"Anything else?" I asked, hopeful she'd keep whatever was bothering her to herself.

"Well…"

I sighed, wiping my palms on my dress pants. "It's okay, Dar."

She met my gaze and nodded. "Roger is on line one."

My jaw clenched as a wave of nausea hit me. I balled my hands, fisting my pants and holding on until I could swallow the bile. My tongue stuck to the roof of my mouth. I stole a deep breath, then another. Finally, the rusty hinges of my jaw loosened enough for me to mutter, "What the hell does he want?"

"He's been holding since the last time I told you he called." She glanced at her watch. "That's three hours or so."

"Really?" I'd figured Roger was desperate, but I couldn't believe he'd waited, listening to our answering loop, for three hours.

"Fine." I waved her off. "I'll get rid of him." The door closed behind Darlene with a snick. I stared at the blinking light, debating whether to talk to him or pick up the receiver then immediately slam it back down.

*Great idea, genius. He'd just call back and guilt you with his ruptured eardrum.*

It would serve him right. But hurting him, while justifiable, wasn't what I intended to do. Now my twin, Roni…

*You can drop kick that biotch off a cliff.*

The corners of my mouth lifted in an evil smirk. I squared my shoulders. If I could broker multimillion dollar international trade agreements, surely I could talk to my ex-fiancé.

I lifted the handset to my ear and pushed the button.

"Hello." I breathed, using the tone that had gotten me the nickname Ice Queen at Warsaw Industries.

"Vanessa don't hang up, please," Roger begged.

"I have nothing to say to you." I swiveled in the chair, glancing out the window at the swelling rain clouds.

"I know. I understand. Please, all you need to do is listen." He paused.

"You've got one minute, Roger," I acquiesced.

*Why give the louse a single second? It won't change your mind.*

"I'm sorry. I don't know how many times I have to say it." He sucked in a breath. "I thought she was you."

Hit with an overwhelming sense of déjà vu, I

wondered how many times had I had this conversation? Different men, same sister.

"I wouldn't have… if I would have known…" Roger stammered.

"I know," I fired back with venom.

"I'm sorry," he uttered again. "I didn't know it was Veronica."

"You slept with her. Just because you believed it was me doesn't make you less guilty. You had sex with my sister. In my office. On my desk." Breathing became difficult, so I leaned back and focused on the overhead lights.

"But I thought I was making love to you," he said in a small voice.

I snapped forward, righteous indignation coursing through my veins. "It boils down to this: you didn't love me enough to be able to tell the difference between my twin and me." Trying to ward off the tears, I shook my head.

Roger's heaving, rapid breaths reminded me of the afternoon I'd found Roni straddling him. I rubbed my temple, anger flaring anew. First, I had remained frozen at the doorway, but when Roger moaned my name, I flew into a rage and attacked my twin. Roni flew off the desk, frog legs in the air, as Roger gasped like a fish out of water while holding "major wood."

*More like a Webelo. Get it? Wee below.*

Thank God, I hadn't had more than a few petting sessions with him, but it was enough to learn that tidbit about the good little soldier who was gung-ho to salute when we kissed.

*Roger has gone-ho instead.*

Call me pusillanimous in my relationships, but I never wanted to share a man with Roni. Usually, I didn't have long to wait before Roni swept in and seduced any would-be life partner my father had introduced me to.

"It's okay, Roger. You're not the only one she's done this to. They've all told me they couldn't tell us apart either: the hardworking twin versus the slut. It's understandable."

*Ah honey, you let the bitterness seep in a little bit.*

"It's not okay," he mumbled. An awkward stretch of silence punctuated the conversation. "I made a mistake."

*Ya think?*

"She always gets them to make the same mistake. Nobody sees me, just a wanton pair of boobs and a vagina." I pinched my nose and sighed. "I can't, Roger. This betrayal, whether intended or not, stabbed my heart." I paused, then added. "It's over. Please don't call again."

I hung up without waiting for a reply. Wringing my hands, I closed my eyes.

# CHAPTER THREE

I WALKED UP THE SIDEWALK toward my front door.
It appeared secure, but the niggling feeling wouldn't
go away. The wreath still hung on the door, but the
red bow now sat catawampus. It had been perfect
that morning. The wind probably moved it. I
scrubbed my face and tried to shake the paranoia.
My sister had no reason to spy on me.

*But that never stopped her before.*

As I entered my home, my supposed sanctuary, I
glanced around. The cat's food and water dishes still
resided by the door to the garage.

I smirked, remembering how Roni had thought
she'd let the cat escape. "You shouldn't be in here,"
I'd stated.

"When did you get a cat?" Roni had asked.

I hadn't, but the neighbor had asked me to cat-sit
their kitty. At the time, they hadn't gone on the trip

yet, but I'd planned ahead. Roni had been more cautious afterward, so I left the dishes even after the cat had returned home.

The house appeared to be unviolated by my sister.

Western light filtered through the blinds in my home office. Dust motes danced lazily about as I inspected the room. The nagging feeling returned.

The pile of paperwork on the desk hadn't been tampered with. Or had it? I opened my phone's photos and scrolled through until I found the picture of the office I'd snapped that morning.

"Ah ha!" The top envelope had been picked up and returned to the pile upside down. Junk mail from a local realtor pitching a house upgrade and credit card offers had been left in plain sight to throw Roni off. I'd taken the plastic cards and cut them up in case Roni would have been tempted. Not that she needed the money, we have plenty of it, but when did having what she needed ever stop her from trying to screw up my life?

Disgusted she'd touched my things…

*Again. Call the sheriff.*

I grabbed the papers and wadded them into a ball. Time to recycle.

A tinkle like wind chimes sounded behind me. I jumped, spinning to face the closet. As I reached for the handle, the door burst open.

"Hello, Prissy," Roni said, stepping out while flipping her long hair. "You've got that nervous tic twitching your jaw again."

I clenched the ball of waste so I wouldn't strangle Roni. My gaze focused behind her into the depths of my closet. The hangers still chimed as they continued to bump into each other. On the floor, my new luggage had been opened and remained askew.

"Get out." I pointed toward the door.

Roni puckered her shiny, cherry-red lips in a pout. "Didn't you miss me?"

I rolled my eyes. "Not on your life," I laughed dryly.

"Are you going on a vacation?" Roni thumbed over her shoulder toward the molested suitcases.

I heaved a sigh and maneuvered her toward the door. "Yes."

Her eyes widened, just a tad. I had piqued her interest. "Dr. Who is stopping by in the Tardis. He's going to take me to an alternate universe where there are no evil twins."

Roni's eyes narrowed. "Then you'd cease to exist," she huffed as she twirled and stomped into the hall.

I followed, making sure she didn't touch anything else, but she stalked straight to the front door and exited into the twilight. On the street, her red BMW's engine revved to life. She flipped me off as she turned around in my driveway.

I locked the door, wanting to slide down it and cry. My lips trembled with an overwhelming feeling of violation.

My soft leather sofa called to me. I meandered over and plopped down, stretching out. On the coffee table, I spotted the brochures for vacation destinations I'd strategically left out. Someday I'd love to take a Rhine River cruise, visit the European castles, trek the Outback, or see the Great Wall of China or Mount Fuji. Inside the Australian trifolded advert, I'd hidden a pamphlet for a hotel in Bern.

I closed my eyes and smiled. Roni had to have seen the red herring pamphlet. The Bern brochure would cause much internet surfing tonight. What could Roni do, really?

*Why ask such things? You know what she's capable of.*

The Swiss hotel belonged to the Tanner Hospitality Group. One of the many international hotels owned by Nick's family. Nicholas Arlington Tanner…

*What a hottie.*

I sighed, wiping a tear away. Nick had been my first love. The only man who'd been able to see the differences between Roni and me.

Roni had told my father something to make him

dislike Nick, and before we could work things out, my mom's cancer took a turn for the worse. Then she died.

Dad never explained why he'd banished Nick from our home. And when I had asked Roni, she'd only shrugged and offered an evil smirk.

Nick had been a super cute, shorter, slightly nerdy guy with cerulean eyes and dark hair. His glasses couldn't detract from his brilliant blue eye color.

Our mothers had been sorority sisters and when they reconnected on social media, they knew they had to meet again in person. Both women had married men with international family businesses, one in manufacturing and the other in hospitality. Both women also had a set of identical twins. Nick was a twin, too.

No use pining over Nick. It'd been nearly nine years since we'd been together. He'd be married with kids by now.

"What to do this evening? Watch the security footage to see where Roni ventured or skim the proposal Daddy wants me to look over?" I hummed, tapping my chin.

The remote lay on the coffee table, tempting me. I sighed. "Fine. It's time for the skank-ho picture show, then some light bedtime reading." My dry laugh echoed through the room, catching in my throat.

# CHAPTER FOUR

SATURDAY, I MADE IT TO the post office before they closed. The small key to my post office box hung on a bracelet with other charms. Hopefully, my hidden-in-plain sight tactic would continue to work on my sister.

I glanced around the lobby. Seeing no one I knew and no one studying me, I put the key in the hole and twisted. The door swung open with a creak. I'd opted for the medium-size box instead of the small. Some goods I'd ordered wouldn't have fit in the small. Even though I knew they'd hold the items for me, but I didn't trust them to distinguish me from my sister, despite the repeated warnings I'd given the clerks at the counter.

A few white envelopes littered the floor of the small cubby. I sifted through them, but my package hadn't arrived yet. I sighed. Hopefully, by Monday.

The rest of the weekend, I focused on perfecting the proposal. Tightening up the verbiage while clarifying it.

Monday, after a telemeeting with our European branch, I walked to my temporary office. As I rounded the corner, Darlene gasped and stared at me wide-eyed. She jumped to her feet, stumbling over her apologies.

I shook my head, putting a finger to my lips.

Darlene nodded and lowered to her seat, biting her lip.

"Call security," I breathed through clenched teeth.

She reached for the handset while I grabbed the door handle. Trying to quell the anger simmering under the surface of my pseudo-calm facade, I closed my eyes and inhaled, the cool metal of the knob a stark contrast to the fire burning within me. After counting to ten to clear my head, I opened my eyes and twisted the knob.

*Let's get that scheming biotch.*

Squaring my shoulders, I donned my Ice Queen persona. I entered quietly but with confidence and my head held high. My goal was to ignore Roni and keep her from seeing any emotion. She'd attemped to mimic my work clothes, and now she sat at the desk, staring at the computer screen with a small smirk on her candy red lips.

She hadn't noticed my arrival. Hopefully, I could

scare the bejesus out of her.

I was halfway to the desk before Roni glanced up. A hand flew to her throat, and the smirk grew into a full-blown sneer.

Rounding the desk, I stopped beside Roni. I crowded her space, hoping she'd get the hint. On the computer screen, the homepage of the airline website I'd visited glared.

"Going somewhere?" Roni asked, blinking innocently.

I crossed my arms as I met her gaze. "Would you get out? I've got work to do."

Roni blew hair away from her face as she stood. "If you won't tell me, I'll ask Daddy."

Now it was my turn to sneer, but I refused to answer. I commandeered the desk chair and tapped on the computer keyboard. I pulled up the meeting notes.

"This explains a lot," Roni declared. "The luggage. The destination mail. You are going on a trip."

I kept pretending to read the notes while keeping Roni in my periphery. Her complexion shifted through shades of pink to crimson.

"I will find out," she grumbled.

I snickered, and she snorted. Roni remained off to the side, staring at the screen, but I couldn't belie my mission.

A knock sounded at the door. "Ms. Warsaw."

Both Roni and I answered. "Yes?" The men in

navy security uniforms glanced at each other then at my sister and I. Mr. Michaels, who was a retired police officer, and a younger man I hadn't met yet moved into the room.

"Get her out of here," I ordered.

Roni crossed her arms in a huff. "Fine. Just wait until Daddy hears about this," she threatened.

*That's the classic "I'm telling" Roni, for you.*

"Please, make sure Veronica is escorted to her car and leaves the property." I swung my gaze to Darlene as she waited behind the men. "Dar, please get Samuel Dumont for me."

Darlene hesitated a moment before asking, "Your lawyer?"

"Yes. Advise him I'd like to talk about filing a restraining order and ask about criminal trespass."

She nodded, making a note on her tablet. "Anything else?"

"I need to speak with Todd Landers ASAP."

"Is your computer acting up?" Darlene's gaze followed Roni as she was led away.

"No. Our system may have been breached."

"Oh, lord," Darlene gasped. "You don't think…"

Roni slapped her palm on the door frame, halting the security posse. "I didn't mess with your computer," she tossed over her shoulder.

I narrowed my gaze. "I don't know what you're capable of, Roni. Todd will examine the network and extra security measures will be installed. Again."

"They haven't stopped me yet," she taunted.

"That's why I mentioned the criminal trespass and restraining order. Mr. Michaels, see that you complete a detailed report."

"Yes, Ms. Warsaw." He nodded and motioned for Roni to continue.

"She's not allowed in this building after what she's pulled." I heaved a deep breath. "If you see her again, call the police."

The men acknowledged me, nodding as they exited with Roni. Darlene held the door, watching the hallway. Before she closed the door, I heard Roni say, "You know, Mr. Warsaw is my father. He's not going to like this one bit. Maybe we can make a deal…"

I rubbed my temples, then rolled my shoulders. Within moments, Todd arrived to give my computer a once-over. He ran tests while I paced.

"How does she keep learning my password?" I asked, turning to Todd.

Hands on the keyboard, he glanced up, then back at the screen. "The network is secure. Do you write it down where she can find it?"

With my hands on my hips, I shook my head fervently. "I learned long ago not to leave my passwords, or anything of value, laying about where Roni could find them."

I wanted to stomp my foot and yell, but Todd

was not to blame. Who *is* to blame is chronicled in the journals I've kept throughout the years. Most of what I'd written revolved around my sister's shenanigans. I had stacks of journals hidden away, with maybe enough evidence to get me out of jail if I snapped.

Todd tapped the keyboard. "Looks like she was on a fishing expedition and only had time to restore and pull up your browsing history."

"Great." I threw my hands into the air. What had she gleaned about my escape?

"Do you want me to clear the cache?" Todd sat up, fingers poised.

"It's fine. What's done is done." I hugged myself. "How did she get access?"

Todd turned and studied me a moment then glanced around the room. "If it's not a malicious program, it's got to be something else."

*Genius.*

I spun and glanced up at the small bubble hiding a camera. "You don't think…?"

"Highly unlikely, but—"

"With Roni, completely plausible." I rubbed my temple again, trying to stave off the headache. I couldn't imagine Roni wasting her time scouring footage from Warsaw Industries' bank of security cameras. It was more likely she'd bribed someone on the security team with money or sex.

"Todd, I want access to the cameras from this computer. I want to see everything."

He grinned at the challenge. He laced his fingers, then stretched his arms, cracking his knuckles.

As his fingers tip-tapped over the keyboard, I leaned against the window frame and turned my gaze heavenward. The sun caressed my face, reminding me that soon, very soon, I'd be flying away. I daydreamed about sunshine, waves, a balmy breeze, and sitting alone on the sand.

"Ms. Warsaw?"

Pulled from my fantasy, I sighed. "Yes?"

"I've got it up."

"See if you can locate my sister on the premises." I moseyed to the desk as the rooms flashed onto the screen then disappeared. Once he'd cycled through the building, he started on the exterior. "Stop," I cried.

The screen showed the parking lot full of empty cars lined in rows from the front angle. He shifted to a second camera, showing the same area from another perspective. "Can you zoom in?"

"Yep." He tweaked the picture, enlarging the couple on the screen.

"Son of a… That little floozy," I muttered. Roni and the young security guard who had escorted her out of my office leaned against my Mercedes. "Can you record this?"

"Can do." Todd minimized the footage for a second.

I lifted the phone and dialed security. "Mr. Michaels, my sister hasn't left the property yet."

"Bosko walked her to her car," he replied.

"I'm watching them in the parking lot. They are at my car, not hers."

"What? I'll take care of it." He ended the call.

Todd and I watched as Bosko jumped to attention, then talked into his radio. He glanced around, spying the cameras. Bosko swallowed, pushing Roni's hands away. She pouted when he turned and stalked toward the building.

Roni cupped her hands over her eyes as she leaned to inspect the passenger side of my car. I laughed. I'd left the edge of a Mediterranean cruise pamphlet peeking out from under the coffee shop trash on the seat.

Roni straightened with a small smirk and practically skipped to her red BMW.

# CHAPTER FIVE

RONI'S RED BEEMER SPARKLED IN the sunlight as I pulled into the post office's parking lot. I heaved a sigh. Roni had to be up to something.

*Red alert.*

A woman holding three priority boxes approached the entrance and an older gentleman held the door open. She ducked in with a broad smile. Customers entered, others exited. When the woman came back out sans boxes, I released the steering wheel and sucked in a cleansing breath before getting out of my car.

Fingering my bracelet with the post office box key, I bolstered my mental armor. The building's stale air swirled toward me as I pushed the outer door open. I glanced through the next set of glass doors and saw Roni batting her lashes and grinning at an older postal worker named Charlie. I hurried to the right, out of her line of sight.

The narrow corridor held rows of little post office box doors, each with a number. The larger boxes, like mine, were at the far end of the room.

I opened the door to my box to find a large packing envelope filling the space. I swallowed my squeal of glee. The sandals had finally arrived. The last piece in my vacation wardrobe puzzle. As I slid the package out, a flat rectangular box the size of a phone dropped to the ground.

The return address was for the Quiet Sort Co.

"I'd forgotten these were coming," I mumbled, picking up the box. "Awesome."

Noise canceling earbuds for the plane and the cruise. I'd ordered them six months ago, and they'd been backordered.

The only other mail was another vacation pamphlet about Rome. I placed it on the top, in case Roni saw it.

I stuck my hand in the box one more time, searching for anything along the side. A breeze stroked the back of my hand as air was sucked into the box when its back door opened. I peered in, seeing the man who'd been talking with Roni. He blinked as I dangled my bracelet with the key.

"I told you my sister would try to deceive you, Charlie."

"Holy crap. She's not… she said…You were right. I'm sorry," he stammered.

Sparks of anger sizzled along my frayed nerves.

Counting to ten should lower my blood pressure or at least give me time to think. I couldn't afford to lose my cool now.

*You can afford a good lawyer. Don't be afraid…*

I shifted the mail and abruptly closed the door. I stalked through the corridor toward the lobby, my younger twin in my sights. As a red-faced Charlie reappeared, I pushed open the glass door.

Roni's eyes narrowed on Charlie when she noticed his empty hands. She licked her lips and plastered on her most seductive smile.

Roni's lips parted.

"Hi Charlie, I got the package today." My loud tone reverberated off the walls and ceilings. All eyes focused on me. I swallowed and forced a smile. A long queue waited behind my sister. Charlie's coworker, an older woman with a bouffant hairdo, did a double take.

Roni's nose crinkled but other than that she remained calm. She put her hands on her hips.

I lifted the larger envelope and waved it. "I shouldn't have worried."

"I'm glad it came," Charlie replied, adjusting his collar. He nodded, and his gaze slid from me to Roni.

Her lips now puckered in a pout. As I readjusted the packages, I positioned the Rome vacation pamphlet on the bottom. It flopped with only one finger holding it.

Roni caught sight of it and her lips twitched.

Stepping closer to Charlie, I said, "I warned you. When I first asked about the box and every time I've visited since, I warned you." I shook my head.

Charlie studied his shoes. "You did, Ms. Warsaw."

"Tampering with mail is a felony, right?" I asked, using my Ice Queen pipes.

"I didn't steal—"

"Charlie, you're welcome to call the police. She was trying to defraud us." I glanced at the ceiling. "Whatever you see fit. I'll testify in court."

With her hands on her hips, Roni tossed her hair. "Listen, Vanessa. Who do you think—"

"No, you listen." My mind reeled. Everyone gazed at me. Words stalled, and Roni's lips quirked into a smirk. "So, how's that STD?" I blurted.

Wide-eyed, Roni's jaw dropped, and her cheeks blazed crimson. The customers stared at my sister, a few whispered to each other.

I stifled a giggle as I backed out of the door. Turning to flee, I let the pamphlet fall.

I waited by my car until I saw Roni huffing and puffing as she marched outside with a pinched expression that meant war.

*That's not good.*

As she spotted me, she squeezed the Rome

brochure in a clenched fist.

Making a show of tossing the packages into the backseat, I waved. I ducked into the car and sped away, hoping she wouldn't follow.

After returning home, I carefully pried open a corner of the earbud bubble mailing package and slid the slender product box out. After resealing the mailer, I returned it to the backseat of my car. If Roni would somehow get inside my car, at least I could piss her off again when she'd open an empty package.

The doorbell rang, distracting me from my scheming. I glanced through the peephole before opening the door. My realtor, Johny, greeted me with a smile.

"Afternoon, Van." A dimple appeared on his right cheek. "We've got company." He nodded his head to the left, indicating my sister… spying.

I sighed. "I'm sorry."

"This is serious. You should go to the police." Johny crossed his arms and grimaced.

"Just act like you're pitching a sale." I stepped onto the concrete pad of the patio and glanced both ways.

"I worry this—" Johny waved his hand around as if shooing a fly, "sister situation could escalate."

"Hand me your card, and we'll meet at the coffee shop like we talked about."

"Fine." He fished a card out of his wallet and

offered it. "I parked on the street like you insisted—
"

*For good reason.*

"And I'll visit your neighbor, too." Johny glanced at his watch.

"She's probably home, and they just moved here a few months ago so you won't get stuck there long." I crossed my arms as if impatient. Another ruse.

"Honey, if I can make another sale, I don't care how long she keeps me." He winked then sashayed away.

Johny, a gay realtor, was a business associate who had become much more. He supported me and my endeavor to escape and was eager to help me put the kibosh on Roni's villainous ways.

He straightened his shoulders as he strutted down the sidewalk to my neighbor's house. I backed into the house, closed the door, and jogged up the stairs, taking them two at a time. Using one eye, I peered out from behind a curtain as Johny engaged in an animated conversation with my neighbor.

I returned to the garage and opened the overhead door. As I drove, I studied my rearview mirror. Would Roni try to get in my house, or would she follow me?

*Why the hell doesn't she get a life?*

I parked on the street between a bookstore and a clothing boutique I frequented. She hadn't followed. At least, not that I had seen.

It seemed Roni had chosen to search my house for the packages. I'd stowed the boxes under the sink, precariously positioned on the waste pipe of the disposal. She wouldn't see them if she opened the door and glanced in.

I grinned as I entered the front of the boutique, then exited out the rear. My destination was in sight at the end of the alley. With each step, more weight seemed to lift from my shoulders. By the time I pulled the door to the coffee shop open, it was as if I'd traded my shoes for helium balloons.

Johny met me at the counter. "I'll have a chai latte."

My brow rose in a Spock-like manner. "I see you still have both ears."

Johny rolled his eyes. "Yes. She's a talker all righty."

I ordered our drinks, then we found a table. I sat where I could watch the entrance. Johny tilted his head, inspecting me.

"You haven't been sleeping well." He frowned. "We've got to get you out of here, girl."

My eyes filled, and I glanced down at the napkin, willing the waterworks away. My hair shifted, hiding my face. The barista called my name and Johny retrieved our order, giving me a chance to tuck my emotions back into the recesses of my heart.

After setting the cups down, he returned to his seat, rubbing his palms together. "Now let's get this show on the road. I've got figures for you to look over. Everything is fine. Everything will work out, don't you worry. Johny is on the case."

I glanced at the paperwork and sipped my latte. Joy buzzed under all my thoughts and emotions, but I wouldn't let it take root. Not yet. There was too much that could go wrong.

"Hello? Van, are you listening to me?" Johny's eyes narrowed.

"Daydreaming about paradise," I mumbled.

He waved his finger. "I'm not buying it. Your expression was haunted by your damn sister." His sympathetic eyes narrowed. "I can't wait until she attempts to bat her eyelashes at me. I'll be all like 'uh uh, honey, you ain't got what it takes'. Or maybe I should lead her on like she's making progress, then drop the lack-of-a-dick comment."

I couldn't contain a snort of laughter. "Whatever you choose, please record it."

My phone chimed. I glanced at the text with a sigh.

"Is it Delilah?" Johny asked, glaring at my phone.

"Delilah?"

"You know, the seductress?"

"That's an apropos name." I grinned. "No, but

almost as bad. It's my father setting me up on a business—" I used air quotes as I continued, "—date."

"Your family." Johny shook his head.

*I know, right?*

He patted my hand as the tears came back and forced their way out. Johny rounded the table and pulled me into a tight hug. "You only need to hold on until Friday, then you're free. You can do it, Van. Freedom is less than five days away." He rubbed soothing circles on my back.

"I wish I could take you with me," I sighed.

He chuckled, vibrating me. "I'd go for the speedos."

"Oh, my God."

"Actually, I need to stay and thwart your family. Remember?"

"Yes," I said, pulling away and dabbing my eyes. "I'm going to blame Roni sending multiple business representatives to my house."

Johny returned to his seat and reached under the table. He pulled out a bag. "That reminds me. Here's all those cards I told you I collected. These are all legit businesses."

I peered into the bag and gasped. "Wow. Thanks."

Johny flashed a toothy grin. "I did good."

"Yes, you did." I nodded. "I almost wish I had

more time to mess with Roni."

He snorted and leaned over the table. "No, you don't."

*What he said.*

# CHAPTER SIX

RONI'S RED BMW WASN'T WHERE she usually parked in the curved drive in front of her house. I pulled around back toward the garage, where my car would remain out of sight.

She must be on a Tuesday afternoon shopping spree with my father. "Guilt shopping" Roni called these sprees he took us on, since we couldn't go with our mother.

Roni's housekeeper, Mrs. Rodriguez, opened the door for me. "Come in, Vanessa. I found several red dresses, but I wasn't sure which one you were looking for." She motioned me in.

We moved through the hallway toward the stairwell. Mrs. Rodriguez's phone rang. She glanced at the screen and sighed. "In her room." She put her finger to her lips to silence me then answered the phone. "Hello, Ms. Warsaw. Everything is going well." She paused, meeting my eyes. Her brows rose then her gaze lifted to the top of the stairs.

I waved and took the steps two at a time. Glancing over the banister, I heard, "That sounds like a lovely necklace, Ms. Warsaw," before I walked out of earshot.

I flicked on the wall switch and illuminated Roni's plush bedroom. The walls were a pale, almost-white pink and the king size bed had enough frilly pillows for an army. I hurried to the other side of the wide room, into a walk-in closet about the same size as her bedroom.

"How many shoes does one person need?" I mumbled, staring at a wall of shoes organized by style, the majority being stilettos.

I eyed the garments and sighed. I didn't have all day, and that's what this task amounted to. Sliding the hangers to the right one at a time, I inspected my brazen sister's skimpy dresses. They were sorted by color, starting with black.

"Geesh. You have enough cocktail dresses to outfit the tabernacle choir. Twice."

If it weren't present day, I'd have thought they'd named the cocktail dress in her honor.

*The cock gets the tail.*

I glanced at the blues, greens, and yellows, then the reds. As I pushed one, I gasped. It was identical to one of mine. This wasn't Roni's taste. It was actually knee-length and not mid thigh, with a slight split at the right leg.

While it was a V-neck, it would only expose some cleavage instead of all cleavage, like she normally wore.

*Classy cleavage.*

I glanced at the brand. "That's the same. Huh." I flipped the tag and gasped. I'd gone to initialing everything I owned and low and behold, it was my dress. That little thief. She'd rummaged through my closet and took it.

*Biotch.*

Now I wanted to check every item, but I didn't have the time.

A car honked. Hugging the dress to me, I hurried to the window in the closet. Roni motioned to whomever she'd honked at.

Great. I had to get out of there. The last thing I needed was a confrontation with the saboteur. I snagged a pair of heels from the lower cubby and crept toward the back stairwell. At the bottom, I peered around the corner into the kitchen.

Roni's voice singsonged as she placed two enormous shopping bags on the counter. "Look at this gorgeous outfit. Isn't it adorable?"

I slunk back and waited, hoping she wouldn't look out the back window and see my car.

"Yes, Ms. Warsaw," Mrs. Rodriguez said.

"I love this color blue and just had to have it. It reminds me of…" Her voice trailed off.

Mrs. Rodriguez brought her back. "What time is your dinner tonight?"

"Seven. Like I told you before," Roni snipped.

"Will you wear this new turquoise dress?"

"I don't know. I wish I knew what Vanessa was wearing."

Mrs. Rodriguez sighed. "Be yourself. You are both beautiful young women."

"Ah, thanks, but we're twins, and I like to do the twins thing."

I stealthily checked around the corner in time to see Roni grab her bags and slide out of the room. Once I suspected she was headed upstairs, I hustled out and handed Mrs. Rodriguez a hundred-dollar bill. The older woman stuffed it into her shirt and waved.

I ran to my car and left, hoping I'd gone undetected.

At Cal's salon, I felt welcomed. Two of his employees worked on me while he trimmed my hair and then styled it in a way to make it look like I had layers. His plan was to pull part of it up to cascade along the sides of my face.

Tami and Dayle massaged my hands and feet, then prepped my nails for polish.

"Come back on Friday, and we'll give you something fun for your trip. This is a temporary fix to help confuse your sister," Cal said conspiratorially.

"I'd like to do something I'd never do for now and get something practical for then," I suggested. "What's your ugliest color?"

Tami smirked. "Let's do an ombre of two colors."

"Do it," Dayle prompted.

Tami hopped up and hurried away. When she came back, she wore an evil smirk. "If you don't mind a creepy color combo, then I propose something like this." She held up a picture of nails with orange fading into black, like a Halloween design.

"What color are you wearing tonight?" Cal asked as he snipped.

"A blood red dress."

"Is that so? If you kill your sister, then the blood will be camouflaged." Tami giggled.

"That's an idea," I laughed, but it fell flat. "I don't really want to kill her, just get away from her. But black and red nails are very different from my norm. This will get her going on its own, let alone the slinky dress and CFM heels."

"CFM?"

I squirmed in the seat as heat blossomed on my face. Clearing my throat, I said, "Come, you know, rhymes with duck, me shoes." I shrugged.

Cal firmly straightened my head.

"Your toes are going black too," Tami declared.

"I'm at your mercy." I said, closing my eyes and relaxing back. "I appreciate what you're doing."

"Revenge makeovers are our favorite," Dayle admitted. And Tami nodded.

"You know, Cal, my evil twin will want to come in here to get her hair done."

"Send her in. I'll give her the true version of your *haircut*." Cal's eyes narrowed as he chuckled.

But Cal didn't understand Roni. "She'd pretend to be me. She convinces everyone. Then once you think she's me, she cajoles you into telling her everything we've done here and why."

Tami stared at me with wide eyes. "Really?"

"Really."

"Girl, you definitely need a vacay," Dayle sympathized.

"Don't worry. I've got it all planned." I hoped.

"I've heard about your departure." Cal said, gently curling a strand of hair.

"On Friday, you'll get the full mani-pedi when you come." Tami grinned. "Maybe you'll find a man while you're away."

"Yes, a tan man with abs and an ass that won't quit." Dayle met my eyes then winked.

"Won't quit what?" Tami asked.

"Use your imagination," I said, glancing at her.

Cal turned my head straight. "Hold still."

As they worked on me and built the perfect vacation man, my thoughts drifted to Nick Tanner. He was perfect for me, at least he had been earlier, before my life turned pathetic.

Chestnut brown hair, deep blue eyes framed with killer lashes and stylish Clark Kent-type glasses, kissable lips, and a sweet smile and best of all… he could tell me and my sister apart by looking at us.

Nick understood me. He'd sacrificed to be there for me when my mother died, and I'd be forever grateful.

The resort where I had chosen to hide from the world belonged to the Tanner Hospitality Group. I knew it would be a well-maintained property, given the family's care of their business locales.

Nick's mother and I corresponded via snail mail a few times a year. General information, no Nick details, but she had reminded me of the Dancing Winds resort when she last wrote. She mentioned it as a secluded getaway.

On the other hemisphere. The opposite side of the world. I couldn't wait to sit on the beach listening to the waves and feel the balmy breeze fluttering through my hair.

No worries. No matchmaking. And, best of all, *no sister*.

Cal poked my shoulder. "Vanessa, hon, Johny is on the phone."

*Daydreaming about Nick and escaping… again.*

"Thanks, Cal." I took the receiver. "Hello?"
"Thank God, Van. Your sister is a real piece of

work, you know that," Johny huffed.

My stomach churned and grumbled as if I'd been sucker punched. Squeezing my eyes shut, I groaned. "What has she done now?" I hit the speaker button. "You're on speaker, Johny."

"Lovely. Hi everyone. Just wait until you hear this. She came by your house while we were there moving furniture and tried to get in. Luckily, Hans stopped her—"

"You have a security guy named Hans?" I stifled my surprise.

"No, hon. Well, yes, I guess so, in this case. He's a daddy beefcake with all kinds of muscles for heavy lifting. Your sister batted her eyes like she was trying to fly." Something akin to a gurgling noise came through the speaker.

"What happened, Johny?"

"Hans saw her red car and knew we were in for it. He alerted us. We initiated shutdown protocol, stopping her from entering the house. The guys slammed the plumbing truck's backdoor before she could see inside. We closed the garage too."

"Did she suspect anything?"

"She's a weasel. Of course, she did. But she saw the rolls of carpet. When she asked what was going on, Jake informed her you were having a renovation."

"Did she buy it?" I glanced around the group who waited to hear.

"Not really." Johny paused, "Well, until Jake

mentioned you might visit her house. She took off like a bat outta hell." He chuckled. "You'll never believe it, but the cops were sitting outside your street and ticketed her."

"Instant Karma," Tami mumbled, rubbing her hands together.

"Hallelujah, there is a God," I said, glancing heavenward. Cal moved my head, positioning it straight once more.

"Now I'm going to get to work and finish your house before the Delilah comes back."

"She actually went home. She was more concerned with her shopping than an intruder." I glanced at my reflection in the mirror. It didn't look much different yet.

Could I pull off a scam?

The red dress hugged my curves in what should have been a comforting manner, but instead it restricted movement. Because of the high heels, I had to take shorter steps and make sure I was perfectly balanced.

Dayle had plucked my brows and once the girls had seen a picture of my sister's face, complete with her usual ten pounds of makeup, they worked to make me look glamorous like Roni, but more tasteful.

With my hair partially up and the back curled in cascading layers, I looked like a movie star. I tried to channel my inner celebrity, as I drove to the venue.

I parked and entered the lobby. The sparkling chandeliers dangled from the high ceiling, and the wood dado and polished parquet floor gleamed in the light. Click-clacking through the wide hallway, I turned into an open set of double doors. The din rose as I entered. Most of the tables were filled.

Spotting my father talking to a young man my age, I inwardly cringed but outwardly pasted on a smile. Tonight I would emulate my sister.

*Let's see how Vic Warsaw likes having two slutty daughters.*

Daddy glanced in my direction and caught my gaze. His eyes widened.

*He's not used to Roni being punctual.*

I glided up to him. "Hi, Daddy," I said, smirking. After kissing him on the cheek, I inspected the other man in true Roni form. Starting at his thick, raven hair and sultry dark eyes, my gaze then moved to note tanned skin, shoulders held back confidently, a tapered waist, muscular thighs, and booted feet. Nice. Probably custom boots.

Roni would gush over the good-looking man and ask all about him while extending a dainty hand to assess the quality of his shake. But I turned back to my father and said, "I'm getting a drink. Would you like one?"

"I'm fine, honey pie."

My smile broadened. He'd used his nickname for my sister. Score. My walk had a little more bravado as I approached the long, wooden bar. Several people watched a game on the TV, drank, and ate. I sat on an empty stool and crossed my legs, waiting for Kevin, one of the club's regular bartenders, to notice me.

*WWRD? What would Roni do?*

I sat up and leaned over a bit, letting the V-neck do its thing. Waving a bedazzled wrist, I caught Kevin's eye.

I ordered Roni's usual cocktail and flirted with Kevin once he returned with it. The older, gray-haired gentleman next to me asked about my father and his line of work. He began talking, telling me his whole life story. I couldn't stay focused as my gaze kept returning to the young man next to my father.

The man caught me perusing his body and rubbed the back of his neck but didn't appear to skip a beat when it came to speaking with my father. There was a certain freedom in unabashedly staring. What you see is what you get with my sister.

*Speak of the devil.*

Roni tossed her head as she entered. Her hair caught the attention of a table of young men I hadn't noticed since I'd been focused on our father.

I needed to remember that trick, because the young men all followed her with their gazes.

She reached out and touched my father's elbow. Deep in conversation, he jumped. His eyes widened as he gazed hard at her. She wore a red dress whose hem hit her mid-thigh. It was backless and had a plunging V-neck. Her strappy heels were even more slutty.

Dad spoke to her, and Roni gasped and shook her head. Then she scanned the room.

Vic Warsaw had just switched his children. And I loved the way Roni was shifting uncomfortably. Although it also pissed me off that my father would think I'd dress like a country club hooker.

*You did dress like that.*

Fair enough.

Roni found me. Her gaze narrowed. With a predatory grin, she raised a hand and waved to me.

Smoke came out of her ears. Not literally, but I could envision it as she stomped toward me. How does one stomp in CFM heels? I'd never mastered that skill.

"Vanessa, what is wrong with you?" she hissed.

"You can answer that by glancing in the mirror." I said, swirling my drink.

"Bitch," she snapped as she flagged the bartender. "I'll have what she's having."

"No can do," Kevin said. "This lady said you're a recovering alcoholic and shouldn't be drinking."

"What?!" Roni turned as red as her lipstick.

"Just joshing with you," he laughed.

"Oh. Well. Fine." She appeared unsettled as she placed a hand on her throat. Then her eyes narrowed as a slow smirk formed. "In that case, I'll have a red wine. A Cab please."

Kevin poured her a drink and handed it to her. She turned, tossed a sneer over her shoulder, then returned to our father's side. She stood rigidly with her shoulders back and nose high. Was she being me? I snorted.

*Here we go again.*

I tipped Kevin a twenty then excused myself from the older fellow. The cute guy my father was talking to now assessed my sister. She batted her lashes and laughed, and I recalled Johny's words and the visual. Flying.

I took my drink and sidled up to my father. As I arrived, the pause in the conversation lasted long enough for me to insert a very Roni observation. "Kevin told me the special on tonight's menu is to die for." I put emphasis on the "die for." Then I added a cheap giggle.

Roni rolled her eyes, but her lashes fluttered

again. "Wow. Thank you, Kevin."

I fingered the rim of my glass, circling it, as I looked at her through my lashes. "You shouldn't scoff. It's steak. And we know how much you like meat. Especially tube steak."

It was Veronica's turn to snort. "Says the vegetarian." She tipped her glass to her lips.

I tossed my hair like Roni does and twittered. "Everyone knows I'm a meat balls kinda girl."

My father cleared his throat, his cheeks tinged pink. "Okay girls, our table is ready."

"Thank you, Daddy," Roni said as she grabbed my elbow and turned to follow him. "What are you up to?" she hissed in my ear.

I smiled when my father glanced over his shoulder at us. His brow tipped in concern. I replied sweetly, "Your normal BS."

# CHAPTER SEVEN

WEDNESDAY AT THE OFFICE, I strode toward
Darlene with confidence. "Look at my nails." I
stretched my arms toward her and wiggled my
fingers.

Her gaze narrowed. "What meeting did you have
on the eleventh?"

I smiled, grateful she implemented one of our
Roni detection strategies. "The proctologist."

Darlene smirked. "The eleventh of what
month?"

"The eleventh of never." I shivered, at the
thought of going to that particular appointment.

Darlene's smirk blossomed into a full-blown
smile. She hopped to attention. "Good morning, Ms.
Warsaw. Your nails are… different."

"I know." Not wanting to go into the hows or
whys, I continued, "Look at this." I lifted my hand
showing the bandage on my thumb.

"Oh, what happened?" Her gaze drifted from my

digit to my face. A flash of concern crossed her features.

"Don't worry. It's another way to spot Roni." I pulled the bandage free exposing a pink heart against the dark background. "I hid this from her. I know she'll go try and replicate the ombre look. This way you'll know."

Darlene nodded. "Thank you." She sighed and shook her head. "It's such a shame…"

I headed into my temporary office but froze and leaned out again. "I have a car appointment during lunch. I might take longer than I'd planned."

"I hope your car is okay."

Fabricating a story—routine maintenance or making a weird noise… Not wanting to lie, I replied. "I may need a rental."

"Oh no." Her hand flew to her throat. "How terribly inconvenient."

"Also, Dar, I'm planning a surprise trip to see Chuck."

Darlene's eyes widened, and she reached for her pad. "Chuck as in Chuck the head of the European division?"

I laughed. "As in that Chuck, yes."

"When should I schedule the trip and—"

"I've already made the plans. And Dar…" I held her gaze. "Don't tell my father."

Her mouth opened but shut again.

I offered the explanation in my Ice Queen tone, "I have to see what's happening before—"

*You need to crack the whipped cream? Imaginary heads are going to roll?*

I left the threat hang. "I'm clearing my calendar in case I need to book an extended stay."

"Very good. Ms. Warsaw." She glanced at her tablet. "Todd from IT will be here shortly."

"Thank you, Darlene. Allow him in when he comes." I retreated to my desk and worked through all the security questions aimed to keep my sister out. Once Todd arrived and installed the latest device to thwart my sister, I could rest easier. At least, at work.

Opening my quadrillion emails, I worked through them. Mostly putting out fires and delegating projects and concerns to others. Since they had to get used to working without me, might as well help the company as much as possible while I could.

"Knock. Knock." Todd sauntered in with a computer bag strung over his right shoulder.

"Just in time," I smiled, leaning back and rolling my shoulders. "So, my new toy came in?"

Todd grinned and practically skipped over to my desk. Pushing my chair, I rolled away, allowing him room to work. I stood and leaned against the windowsill.

"This shouldn't take long," Todd said, glancing up at me while pulling a small box from his bag. He opened it and lifted the white pad out. Next, he attached it to the hard drive and booted the device. "It's loading."

I perched where I could see the bar on the screen as the installation progressed.

"Will this really stop your sister? She's your identical twin." Todd's concerned gaze studied me for a moment.

I stepped toward him, staring at the thumbprint reader. "Even identical twins have different fingerprints." My gaze snapped to his. "Everyone is fooled by her appearance and lets her in here, but technology may finally protect me."

Todd nodded then returned to his job. After another few minutes a blue light flashed on the side, and he turned toward me. "Ready?"

I placed my thumb on the pad and rolled it side to side reminding me of an iPhone security button.

After Todd left, I leaned back in my chair and crossed my arms. It's a shame I won't be around when Roni attempts to get into my computer now.

*No, it's not.*

Quite right. Only a few more days, and I'm out of here.

I spent my lunch break at the title agency selling my car. Johny picked me up afterward and took me to get the rental I'd reserved.

As we waited for the woman to run the final check on the rental, Johny hugged me. "It's almost time. I'm going to miss you."

I stomped down the waterworks as I returned the embrace with a bear hug. "Thank you for making my escape possible."

He broke the embrace then took my hands. "I'm glad I could help. I'll try my best to keep the ruse up for as long as I can." Johny sighed. "Girl, you need to have a voodoo doll made of your sister."

I chuckled, "If only that would work…"

"All right, Ms. Warsaw, you're all set." The woman dangled the key fob in the air.

"Thank you." Snatching the key fob, I leaned and inspected the little gray Toyota sedan. I waved as the attendant returned to the car rental office.

"Plain and inconspicuous. Just like you wanted," Johny noted, crossing his arms. "That little twat will overlook this car."

"Let's hope so," I mumbled.

"Countdown to vanishing. Go Vanessa." Johny waved an imaginary team flag.

"And reappearing in paradise," I added, jabbing the air with my pointer finger, not wanting to disappear forever. Only long enough for my sister to find her own path and leave me the hell alone.

"Maybe you'll find a hot cabana boy and have the fling of your life." He wiggled his eyebrows.

*Here's hoping…*

"I just want to be alone on the beach. I'm not looking for a relationship."

"Harumph." He rolled his eyes. "Girl, you just need the big D. It's the cure for what ails you."

I snorted. Laughing, I clutched my sides as I doubled over.

"I'm serious. Worship at a phallus your slutty sister hasn't ground down to a nub."

The giggles kept undulating from my gut in waves. "Stop it. I can't breathe."

With his nose in the air, he fluttered his lashes. "Nothing funny about the almighty dick."

I might have snorted again.

*Totally.*

Glancing at the sky, I sobered and sighed. "I hope I can escape without complications."

"She's a royal pain in the ass complication. I can help with that. I know a guy." Johny studied his fingernails.

I turned to face Johny. He was a social butterfly and knew people in all walks of life but… "You know someone who could bump someone off?"

"Not bump off." His brows dipped as he grinned evilly. "Bump against. A diversion. Keep her occupied with a male version of her."

I worked to hide my shock. "A male version?

That sounds intriguing. I almost wish I had time to mess with Roni, but I won't tempt fate."

# CHAPTER EIGHT

My childhood bedroom was exactly how I'd left it when I went off to college. Same white duvet and a rainbow of pillows. Plush animals lined in a row on my chest of drawers.

I sat cross-legged on the bed, staring into the darkness of the walk-in closet. I'd deposited three totes full of personal items into the very back corner, taking care to place a dusty shoebox on top.

I shook my head, making my hair cascade around my shoulders. "What great lengths I deploy to thwart my sister."

There was a time—before I met Nick Tanner and before Mom died—when Roni and I were close.

We used to wear matching clothes and to do the identical twin thing where we switched places in school. Our friends would confuse us, but we rolled with it mostly, until high school, when we started wearing different styles.

"What happened Roni? Why do you hate me so

much?"

I pulled out the end table drawer and found the Bible Grandma had bought me the same day she'd cursed me. Flipping the cover, I gazed upon the face of my first love. Nick smiled back at me, and a warm fuzzy feeling itched at my wounded heart. I'd hidden the special memory within the one place I was sure prying eyes wouldn't find it.

Taking a deep breath, I squeezed my eyes shut. I slipped nick's senior picture into my purse. Somethings I wouldn't leave behind. I willed the tears away then stood.

Glancing around my old room, I wondered if it would be the last time I saw it?

In the hallway, I paused and tossed a last look into the space where I'd spent so much of my youth. A haunting memory washed over me—my mother sitting beside me singing a lullaby while tucking me into bed. She'd been a great mother. I was grateful for the time I'd had with her, but...

*Damn cancer.*

Rolling my shoulders, I walked further away from my childhood with each step. Once in the kitchen, I let the echoes of more memories play out before wiping the tears. I missed making cookies with Mom or sitting and having a cup of tea while talking over life stuff. Our last talks had included Nick. Mom recognized we were meant to be together, but then Roni turned my father against Nick and Mom died before I could resolve anything.

The sky outside turned gray and moody. It was a somber metaphor for my life. As I dug in my purse for my parents' house key, numbness replaced nostalgia. Removing the key, I tossed it into the junk drawer.

The happy family in the pictures on the wall seemed to mock me as I made my way toward the front door. The furniture, picked and placed by my mother, was the same as it had been ten plus years ago. In fact, the only thing new was mine and Roni's college graduation pictures.

My phone vibrated. I glanced at the screen. Darlene had sent a photo of Roni with the same nails, minus the failsafe.

*Gotcha Biotch.*

I hurried to the rental car and raced back to Warsaw Industries. As I pulled into the parking lot, people gathered at the employee entrance. In the center, Roni, one hand on her hip, waved her other arm around like she was at a rave.

Luckily, she'd been distracted by the security detail and hadn't noticed where I'd parked.

Roni's red face matched her car. Her eyelids had to tire as she fluttered her lashes, hoping to get away with whatever scheme she had hidden by her thong.

She tapped her foot. I approached from behind

her, and Mr. Michaels' eyes widened when he noticed me. Breezing past with a wave, I slid my keycard through the slot without making eye contact.

Before the door shut, I heard Roni growl my name. A laugh bubbled out of me. I'd won this round.

Nodding at Darlene as I approached my temporary office, I lifted my hand to show her the nail.

"That was a great idea, Ms. Warsaw. You saved yourself a load of trouble." Darlene stood with her pad and followed me into the office.

The overcast sky darkened the room, and I turned on my desk lamp. It cast a warm glow over the desktop, which had been undisturbed by my sister.

There was a slight disappointment in not having her defeated by the thumb print scanner. But seeing Roni throwing her version of a fit, having been escorted out by security, was priceless.

Darlene whisked through the calls and appointments—ones I'd missed and the ones she'd rescheduled. She had a soothing voice, and I relaxed. Luckily, I'd had the foresight to plan for Darlene's future employment and made arrangements for lateral movement.

*She has an excellent bullshit detector. Not 100%, but hey, it's Roni.*

When I was alone, I glanced through my desk drawers, searching for anything I couldn't live without. I sighed. While I loved my job, letting it go wasn't as hard as I'd thought it would be.

*It could be… you haven't had a decent vacation in ten years.*

Yeah, maybe.

# CHAPTER NINE

FRIDAY, I STRODE INTO THE country club, attempting to act like I wasn't trying to disappear off the face of the planet. As I glanced around the familiar surroundings, I was struck with a strange sensation—equal parts anticipation and regret.

I loved my father and hated to leave him suddenly but, for my mental health, I needed to escape and start over.

"Vanessa," Dad called with a wave. He sat at the bar, nursing what looked like an Arnold Palmer.

"Hi, Daddy." I leaned in and kissed him on the cheek.

His smile grew. He motioned to the man beside him. "You remember Richard Davis."

The gray-haired gentleman nodded. "Hello, Vanessa."

I greeted my father's golfing buddy, AKA shareholder with a handshake. "Who won today?" I asked.

"Today was Richard's day. Next week will be mine," my father replied with a sparkle in his eye.

"Is that how it works, Vic?" Richard laughed.

I chuckled.

"Vanessa, Kyle enjoyed meeting you for dinner. We should all dine together sometime," Richard suggested, standing to leave.

"He's very knowledgeable in his field. I enjoyed our conversation," I offered, although I don't think I could keep focused on Kyle's chipmunk voice again. I kept wanting to huff helium to reply.

*But Roni enjoyed other things more.*

"Have a wonderful lunch." Richard stalked toward the exit.

"Are you hungry?" My father led me to a table, and we took a seat. I tossed a look toward the entrance but didn't expect Roni to waltz in, since this wasn't a matchmaking attempt.

"Sure." Not really. I studied his furrowed brow as he read the menu. His hairline had receded some and his temples were now gray. The lines at the corners of his eyes and mouth were deeper, but for the most part, he'd aged well. He kept active with golfing and charity fundraising as well as Warsaw Industries.

I'd break his heart when I left. He'd be horribly angry and make excuses for my absence until the letter arrived. I'd scheduled the resignation letter to arrive on my thirtieth birthday. It's when the company would turn over to the shareholders. I wasn't worried. We had a great team in place—it would just no longer be a Warsaw's birthright.

*Too bad grandma was a major douche and cursed us.*

My appetite fled, but I glanced down the list of lunch items. My stomach twisted in knots. After we ordered, I relaxed back and let my father ramble on about his golf game. Supposedly Richard cheats.

*More like Vic Warsaw doesn't like to be bested by the squeaky-man's father.*

I'd wager money on the second option. When Dad laughed, my breath hitched. I'd miss that boisterous sound.

"Vanessa, why are you smiling like that?" His bright hazel eyes caught me in their sights. I swallowed back my emotion and sipped my tea.

After clearing my throat, I said, "Your laughing brought a memory to mind. Remember how when we were kids we used to have tickle fights?"

He nodded.

"One time you tickled mom when she had a mouthful of soda and she spit it all over food she was making."

"Yes, I remember. She came after me with a

wooden spoon.”

“I forgot that part.” I began giggling. “Then she started tickling you. Boy, you’re ticklish.”

“She had me squirming on the floor. I couldn’t breathe.”

“Roni and I had to rescue you,” I pointed out with a smile.

Dad rubbed his chin, a wistful grin resting on his lips. He stared into the past. “Good times,” he whispered.

“I miss her,” I mumbled, barely sounding like myself. When she died, I lost more than my mother. I lost my greatest advocate, best friend, and encourager. My isolation began when cancer took her.

Maybe Mom’s absence is why Roni acted out?

*Nah. Roni was a bitch before Mom died.*

True.

Dad covered my hand with his. “So do I, babydoll. Every day.” His watery gaze held mine, and we continued to reminisce about my mother through the meal. It was a fitting conversation, and a much needed one.

I picked at my food while Dad told me about spotting the cute college girl on spring break and their whirlwind nuptials by June the same year. “A match made in heaven…”

My heart ached to have a love like that…

*Honey, your heart just plain aches.*

He glanced up at me, hope in his eyes.

Nope. We are going to stave off trying to fix me up with the next penis to walk in the room.

"Tell me about the first Christmas you were married," I tried, hoping he'd take the bait.

He pressed his lips together before sighing. Then he leaned back and folded his hands in his lap over the white napkin. "Your mom made our stockings. They were her first sewing project since her home economics class. They sucked." He chuckled. "Don't get me wrong. They were better than anything I could make then or now. But they fell apart when we stuffed them."

"Wow. Mom could always sew." I knew a different Vivian Warsaw. I sighed and glanced at my watch.

"Do you have somewhere you have to be?" Dad asked, one brow raised.

"Yes. It's a salon appointment. But I'm having a good time talking about Mom. It helps dull the ache of missing her. Maybe I'll cancel and continue the conversation."

"Sorry, babydoll. I have a board meeting to discuss the local community concert fundraiser." He glanced at his own watch.

We rose, and I hugged him tight, fighting back tears. "I love you, Daddy. Have a great weekend."

"I love you, too." He squeezed back. "I heard you're taking a little time to visit the European branch."

I inhaled. "How did you…?"

"You gave Dave lead on a project you wouldn't give up unless…" he shrugged. "Darlene holds information tight to her chest but, eventually, I got enough out of her to connect the dots."

"Yes, I'm leaving tonight." Incomplete truth bomb.

He took me by the hands and smiled. "I'm glad. A change of scenery will do you good. And it won't hurt to have the big boss show up, either." He squeezed my palms. "You might get lucky and find someone—"

"Dad." I rolled my eyes and pulled away from him, growling. "Give it a rest."

"I'm serious. You never know."

I did. My first love worked in Europe for his family, but there was no way I'd show up without any warning after years apart. I wasn't sadistic enough to want to meet his wife and kids. No. It was better to have Nick Tanner live on in my memory as my sweet first love. First everything—first kiss, first time making love, first man who could tell my twin from me.

*The only man.*

He was too good of a catch to have remained

single after all this time. I wouldn't risk my heart. It was in too fragile of a state already.

# CHAPTER TEN

I PARKED BEHIND THE SALON building but walked to the front entry in a frazzled state. My brain ran scenario after scenario of meeting Nick randomly—on the airline, in the airport, on a train, in Europe, on the cruise ship, and at the resort. What would happen if I saw him again? I stood inside the salon door, shifting from side to side.

"Earth to Van," Johny called, waving his hand in my face.

I blinked.

"Don't go yet. We've got to make you fabulous." Johny smirked.

"What's this we stuff?" Cal asked, crossing his arms over his broad chest.

"Well, I helped get her here," Johny groused.

"Don't fight," I said, softly. "Wait until I'm gone."

"You got it, hon," Johny said. He held up his hand, inspecting his nails. "I could use a manicure."

He met my gaze and winked.

"For you, brother, it will cost double."

"What's double of nothing?" Johny laughed.

"Come on, Vanessa, let's get your pedicure going. You're heading to a new life, and I promised to help start it right." He led me to a station, and I took a seat, dipping my feet in the warm swirling water.

Tami worked on my toes. "How did you do?" She pointed to the failsafe nail.

"Roni attempted to sneak into my office. Luckily, she was caught because of this." Wiggling the painted nail, I smiled, remembering how angry she'd been outside the building.

"Karma." Tami giggled. "Here, soak your nails in this for a few minutes."

I dipped my fingers in the warm solution as she rubbed my feet then painted my toenails.

When she finished, she led me to a manicure station and Johny took the seat next to me. Dayle studied his cuticles, then directed him to soak his hands in warm water.

We chatted as our nails were trimmed and polished. I opted for a French manicure. Something subtle yet classy.

Johny glanced at me with a strange expression.

"What?" I asked.

"I'm envious."

A laugh busted out.

"Not of the why, Van, but that you have the guts

to do it." His wide-eyed gaze met mine. "You are so brave."

I gasped. "I'm running away—you think that's brave?"

"I do. You're starting a new life," Tami said.

Dayle added, "Without the help of family—"

"Or a man," Johny said. "But maybe you'll find one along the way."

I rolled my eyes dramatically. "Ugh. Now you're sounding like my father."

Johny sat up straight and frowned. Dayle tapped the back of his hand. "Stay still."

"Listen honey. I'm not forcing you to wed some moron in order to make the gods happy. Just find something to plug that hole in your—"

"Heart," Tami interrupted when a mom and young daughter walked past toward the pedicure station.

Cal leaned against the glass door, his head swiveling as he scanned the parking lot. "What's he doing? He's been there since I arrived." Curiosity gnawed at my gut.

"He's the lookout for your sister. He's got a plan if she shows up." Dayle's gaze hopped to each one of us then settled back on the nail file.

"That's so sweet," I mumbled through the emotion clogging my throat. In such a short time I had friended an awesome group of people.

"Thank you all for helping me. I'm grateful for your support." I blinked away the moisture in my eyes. "Your encouragement helped me have the courage to make my escape."

"Everything is done with your house now." Johny glanced at the girls then me. His discretion was appreciated, in case someone came looking for me. The less they knew the better.

"Thank you for orchestrating it, maestro."

Johny graced me with a flourish. He had taken care of storing my furniture or selling what I didn't want. All my housewares and left over clothes would be donated to charity. My house wasn't a home anyway, so it was time to let it go.

"All done," Tami said with a smile. "What do you think?"

"Shiny." I smiled.

"It's Delilah," Cal called, hurrying away from the door. "Come on, follow me."

Johny, Tami, and Dayle all jumped to their feet. I scampered after them into the back room.

"I have your suitcase here," Johny thumbed over his shoulder to my bag by the door. He'd taken it from me to hold, so Roni wouldn't find it.

"This is it," I stated.

Johny and the girls hugged me at the same time. I glanced up and witnessed Cal peeking through the back door. "Tami, you're on," Cal ordered.

Tami pulled away with a sigh. "She's such a whiny bitch." At the door, she turned back and waved. "Goodbye. Have a great new life."

Cal took my hands in his. "You've got this.

Don't look back, only forward."

I nodded as a wave of emotion rocked over me.

"I wanted the exact same as my sister," Roni yelled as Tami tried to pacify her.

Cal and Dayle exited, leaving Johny and me alone. He hugged me again. "You're going to be fabulous. And have peace. No demon sister to harass you anymore. I'll help you to your car."

He extended the handle on my luggage with a firm tug. "Let's roll."

"That's not good enough!" Roni shrieked.

Johny dropped the handle and slunk to the doorway. He peaked into the other room then faced me again. He put a hand on his hip and cocked it to the side, tossing invisible locks. Stomping a foot, he wiggled his index finger while appearing constipated.

Roni continued to rant but was muffled when her voice lowered in tone to her version of the Ice Queen.

Johny cocked his hip to the other side, tossing his head again while his mouth opened and closed like a fish.

*OMG. That is SOOO Roni.*

I bit back my laughter and covered my mouth for good measure.

Johny peered out the door again. With a look of disgust and a wave of dismissal, he pivoted and stormed back to me. "I can't believe you share DNA with that—that—that,"

"Bimbo? Biotch? Hussy? Psycho? Loser? N'er do well?" I offered.

"Yes. All the things." He clamped onto the handle again. "N'er do well?" He asked, one brow raised.

"Well… It fits." I shrugged with an apologetic smile.

"Truth." With a shake of his head, he tugged the large suitcase. It rolled easily, but he teased, "Damn, hon, what do you have in here? It weighs like you stuffed an elephant."

"All my sorrows…"

Johny stopped, let go, and twisted around. He pulled me into his arms and engulfed me in his firm embrace. He smelled heavenly, and I burrowed in, ignoring the emotion threatening to crack my heart. Too late. Surrounded by a cocoon of fondness, I let my crumbling defenses fall. A sob bubbled through a crack, followed by another.

It felt good to be held. Touched by someone who cared and supported me.

"Oh you," Johny held me until I quieted.

"I may have ruined your shirt," I hiccuped, wiping the wet spot on his chest.

"I have other shirts. There's only one Van."

My lip quivered as another bout of emotion surfaced. Johny rubbed my back. "Lords and ladies, your family. Look what they've done to you."

Cal strode into the back, shaking his head. He stopped abruptly. "What's wrong?"

I backed away and wiped my eyes. "Saying goodbye is hard."

Cal took my hand. "You will have a great life, Vanessa. You are destined for good things and love, too. Don't look back. Keep moving forward."

I sucked in a breath and nodded. "Thank you."

With a gay man on each side, I finally made it to my rental car. Johny stowed the luggage and Cal held the door open for me. With one more hug from each man, I closed the last door on my old life.

# CHAPTER ELEVEN

SEEING MY SUITCASE DISAPPEAR DOWN the hole as the conveyor sucked it in had me worrying the airline might lose it. It was my life. My new life.

I boarded the Air France flight to Paris and tried to relax in the first class seating. People lumbered up the aisle with carry-ons and children in tow. My earpods played soothing music, but I'd only relax once the plane taxied on the runway without my sister on board.

Once in flight, I settled into a tranquil state while sipping a glass of red wine. Staring out into the clouds, I wondered if my father would send my sister to watch over me or if she'd decide to come torture me on her own. I had measures in place to minimize the chance of that happening, but… with Roni, I always had to watch my back.

I looked forward to alone time in the hotel I'd booked. Of course, I'd purposely picked one belonging to the Tanner Hospitality Group. THG had resort properties all over the world. They weren't as well-known as some of the conglomerates mainly because they bought mom and pop properties and kept the original names while standardizing the quality of service to match their other units.

I doubted Nick would work the front desk of the Paris location. What would I do if I bumped into him?

Swirling the red cabernet, I remembered Nick's cerulean blue eyes and his grin with a slight dimple on the right side.

I finished the wine and refused another. I switched my music to beach sounds. Closing my eyes, I reclined my seat, envisioning my destination. I would cruise for a few days before ending up at the Dancing Winds resort. Palm trees blowing in a balmy breeze and the rhythmic lull of gentle waves. No one around to bother me—my ultimate daydream.

I sighed.

I awoke to the flight crew scurrying around as the captain announced local time and weather. I yawned, rubbing the sleep out of my eyes and restoring my seat to an upright position.

Waiting in the customs line, I worried my suitcase hadn't made it. When I reached the baggage carousel, my worry was for naut, because my silver hard-sided case was the first to topple through. I'd slapped a palm tree sticker on the side to recognize it easily.

I took hold of the telescoping handle and extended it.

"Ms. Warsaw?" a man's deep voice with an English accent asked.

I glanced around to find Chuck Harding, smiling. He stepped forward. "Here, let me take that for you."

"I didn't expect to see you, Chuck." I allowed him to take the handle.

"Your father called to let me know you were coming. He wanted someone here when you arrived." Chuck walked toward the exit.

I shuffled next to him, miffed my father had intervened, yet grateful I didn't have to navigate the city alone.

"Thank you, Chuck," I said, glancing over my shoulder out of habit.

"It surprised me to hear of your visit." He graced me with a sideways glance. "Unscripted visits are usually the sign of drastic changes to come."

"For me, not you," I said.

He jerked to a stop, and I almost tripped on his heel. "What do you mean?"

In my discombobulated state, I almost gave away my plans. Shrugging, I offered, "This is my excuse to have a vacation I can write off. After I visit the company, I'm going off-grid for a while. Take a train through Europe. Country hop. Get a massage or two." No need to explain the countries weren't necessarily European.

"Vic had me worried." Chuck continued toward the waiting car.

We pulled up to the hotel. Before entering, I said, "Chuck, feel free to report I arrived. But, please, keep my plans on the down low. Let's keep everyone on their toes, including my father." I winked.

"Yes, Ms. Warsaw." He grinned conspiringly then waved as he left.

I'd escaped the country. In less than twenty-four hours, I'd travel to Switzerland, where I'd board a direct flight to the Cayman Islands for a planned layover for banking. I scheduled my last flight to arrive a day before the cruise ship would leave port.

I opened my purse. There, nestled between a printout of flights and the Dancing Winds brochure, was Nick's senior picture. His blue eyes reminded me of the sea. He smiled at me, and I recalled his words, "Your life is yours, Nessa. Live it how you want."

I wanted freedom and would take it. The beach called my name.

# EPILOGUE

THE SALTY BREEZE BLEW TENDRILS of my hair free from the French twist. But if the wind whipped my hair into a bouffant, I wouldn't give a rat's ass. The only person I had to please was me.

People, alone and in small groups, stood on the deck, waving and calling well wishes to the boarding vacationers.

The warm air fluttered the dress around my legs, tickling me. The temperature was perfect, and I didn't need anything on my arms.

I'd already dressed for dinner, slipping on the red dress I'd stolen back from Roni. The formal dinner loomed soon, but not before I kept sentinel over the gangway. Well-dressed travelers funneled up the long metal bridge connecting the ship to the land for embarkation.

The longer I'd been away, the more joy replaced suspicion. But still I studied every person who boarded the ship, double checking to make sure Roni hadn't followed me. I leaned against the rail and inspected the faces of those waiting to board. Old habits die hard.

A group of women staggered across. Even from the distance, I could hear their loud shouts and giggles.

"They will make prime people watching," I mumbled to myself.

*As long as it's not that biotch, Roni, we're good.*

A woman in a sleeveless dress and floppy hat, but hair the same color as mine, approached with a bald man in a suit. I held my breath. The spiky heels made the woman taller than the man, who walked with a cane. Roni would do anything to get to me, even be the arm candy of an ancient billionaire.

When she glanced upward, I waved. She waved back, and her underarm flapped. Not Roni.

"Phew," I blew out a relieved breath.

My feet hurt by the time a team finally went to detach the gangway.

At that moment, a white limo pulled beside the walkway. The driver opened the door for a man. He was tall, with a chiseled body, a dark mane of hair, and black sunglasses. With his shoulders back, he stepped as if he owned the world. Even from the distance, I could tell this man always got what he wanted.

*Note to Vanessa: do not attract any more assholes. You've only just ditched your sister. You don't need another one.*

Right.

Aside from the sailors, the man was the last to board. I could breathe easier now and enjoy the voyage.

Instead of the elevator, I took a sweeping grand staircase to the promenade and waded into a throng of people meandering along, following a delectable scent.

The young, handsome maître d' greeted me with a grin. "Good evening and welcome, Ms. Warsaw. Tonight, you're seated with a couple from Wyoming." He gestured toward an older couple, laughing loudly as they clinked glasses of champagne.

I pasted on a fake smile. "Would it be possible to sit alone?" I fluttered my lashes, trying Roni's trick.

"We will accommodate you." He nodded. "Give me a moment to set your table." He motioned to another young, dark-skinned man, and they spoke to each other in a language I didn't recognize. The youth glanced at me then scurried off.

An ornate mirror lined the entry to the dining room. I glanced at it, recognizing the woman staring back as a nomad who chose to run away.

*Because she didn't know how to face the probs*

*without killing her sister*.

I was sad and anxious. My identity had been knotted up with my family and the family business—Roni's identical twin, Vic Warsaw's daughter, and the CEO of Warsaw Industries.

But I'd have time to grieve my old life later. Right now, I was stepping into a new world full of beautiful scenery, good food, excellent drinks, and people I'd never met.

After a moment, I was led to a table for two with only one place setting. I had a window view. As the evening progressed, the murmuring of the guests rose and fell like lapping waves.

For the most part, I kept my gaze trained outside, but occasionally I panned the guests. The boisterous Wyoming couple had no problem making friends. Someone in the group of giggly women spilled a drink and the room's volume spiked.

The vast twilight sky held no clouds. It was as open as my future, and hopefully the stars would sparkle on me anywhere I went. Now that I'd cut the cords and become free, who was I?

The courses were served one at a time—chilled cantaloupe gazpacho, a salad, a roast, and a decadent selection of desserts.

I chose a cheesecake torte with fresh raspberries and strawberries and a fruit sauce drizzled over the plate. I loved the creamy concoction and asked for a piece to go in celebration of my new start.

*Eat whatever the hell you want.*

The server filled my glass with champagne, and the room toasted the voyage. Lifting my glass, I saluted with the others. The champagne had great flavor, and I accepted a second pour.

The alcohol warmed me as I pondered the other guests. The gigglsome women cheered a friend who celebrated a divorce.

A deep laugh rang like church bells, and I twisted in my chair to witness a blond man blush. The deep voice belonged to a black man with an unmistakable Jamaican accent. He continued to tease the blond man.

The blond met my gaze. I gasped like I'd been sucker punched. He reminded me of Nick, complete with his cerulean blue eyes. He offered a sheepish grin before the Jamaican nudged him. I turned away and squeezed my eyes shut, trying to breathe.

*What a cutie. And such a Nick clone. If Nick was buff, blond, and didn't need glasses, that is.*

Shaking my head, I rubbed my face. I'd been reminiscing about Nick, and now I'm paying the consequence. Will I see him everywhere I go?

I needed to purge the past, and that included Nick Tanner. I reached inside my purse and glanced at Nick's picture. The thought of throwing the photo away made my gut churn. No, I'd store it in one of the little-used zip pockets in my luggage.

After dinner, I wandered toward the main deck and glanced over the rail. Could I find friendship and trust again? Could I find hope and love again?

I didn't know. And right now, I didn't want to know.

The water reflected starlight, and a warm, briny breeze caressed me. I'd found freedom. A smile blossomed on my lips.

No more Ice Queen. In a few days, I'd be queen of my cabana.

# Love a book?

## Please leave a review.

## Reviews are virtual hugs for authors.

## THE 24 HOUR BET TEASER

### Learning to Love Again
### Book 2

I traded my career, my inheritance, and my anxiety to bask in the sun at a tropical resort halfway across the world. But I sabotaged my chance at solitude by opening my mouth. I threw my good sense out for a stupid bet.

I have to spend twenty-four hours attached to a man.

What the hell is wrong with me?

Although, losing my privacy is not a total loss because my companion is super hot and reminds me of my first love, Nicolas Arlington Tanner.

What can go wrong in twenty-four hours? And what could go right?

Enjoy a sneak peek of

# The 24 Hour Bet

The Jamaican's laugh rang out, causing me to pause. His head tipped back, and his eyes crinkled in mirth.

Nick's look-a-like wore a sheepish grin. He stuck his hands in the pockets of his khaki pants and waited. I'd witnessed this a time or two on the cruise ship. He'd get teased. He took it good-naturedly and always wore a smile, but it bothered me. I had to force myself to not intervene. But I kept my mouth shut and observed. I sensed a sibling-like relationship, and it seemed to work for them.

They were arguing over a stupid bet. "Money, that figures."

"I'm not going to do that." The Nick look-a-like crossed his arms over his chest and frowned.

Oh, he was manning up. I can't explain why it made my heart race, but I became intrigued. I wanted the underdog to stand up for himself.

The Jamaican leaned toward his friend with a confident smile. "It's because you can't."

"It's not that at all. It's just stupid, Mike."

Good grief. Nick's look-a-like was sexy when he put his foot down. I studied his jawline, his brow, and the width of his shoulder. Shit, I shouldn't be studying him if I am anti-men. And I am *definitely* anti-men.

"It's a thousand dollars." Mike, the Jamaican shrugged, then threw me a look.

"Easy money, but a waste of time. No one will agree to such a thing." He dropped his arms and stuffed his hands into his pockets again.

"Let's ask this young woman." Mike pointed at me and smiled sheepishly.

I rolled my eyes and walked over to them.

"Miss, would you please give us your opinion about a bet?"

My gaze raked the Nick look-a-like. His pale gray shirt was pulled taut over his muscled biceps and chest. He could handle himself in an endurance challenge. If it required flirting, the drunk ladies would be more than willing to comply. Karen certainly needed a boost in confidence.

"What's the bet?" I asked.

The blond's face turned a deep crimson, and I couldn't help but smile. He shook his head.

"All he has to do is spend twenty-four hours with a woman." The Jamaican's smile reached from ear to ear, reminding me of a bearded lizard.

I sized up the American in a new light. He was easy on the eyes and, from what I'd observed on the cruise ship, polite and well mannered. I could almost handle him. Almost. If I hadn't come here to be alone.

"He's right, easy money," I agreed.

"Thanks." Nick's look-a-like grinned. I nodded and turned away.

"But that's not all he has to do," Mike baited.

I turned to face them again. "What else?" I asked, hoping I hid my impatience.

"He has to remain physically attached to her the whole time." Mike stood with his hands on his hips in triumph.

Linking a man and woman for twenty-four hours? It was physically impossible. *Wasn't it*? My mind raced. I didn't know if the American had the stamina for such an activity, but my body liked the thought of trying.

**Romance with Sass & Shenanigans
books by
Rochelle Bradley**

*The Double D Ranch*
*Plumb Twisted*
*More Than a Fantasy*
*Municipal Liaisons*
*Here We Go Again*
*The Playboy's Pretend Fiancée*
*Cole's New Song*
*Brad*
*Canon*
*Destination Escape*
*The 24 Hour Bet*

**Books by Rochelle Bradley & CJ Warrant**
Boba Book Babe Mysteries

*Pandemonium in Peoria*
*Silenced in San Antonio*

**Magic. Mystique. Mischief.
books by
Rochelle K. Bradley**

*Dragonfly Wishes* - Dragons of Ellehcor 1
*Dragunzel* - Dragons of Ellehcor 2

*Descended* - Secrets of the Fallen 1
*Charmed by Murphy* - The Murphy Brothers 1
*Murphy's Paws* - The Murphy Brothers 2
*The Secret Shelf*

# About the Author

Born and raised in Cincinnati Ohio, Rochelle developed a love of nature and art. She is a Bearcat, a Buckeye, an interior decorator, and fluent in sarcasm. She currently lives in southwest Ohio and shares her home with a black cat, a leash trained orange tabby, and her Prince.

Rochelle co-hosts (with author CJ Warrant) Wednesday Coffee & Books an Instagram Live show where they interview romance authors. Watch the show Wednesdays at 11 AM EST.

Rochelle is an award-winning author including three IHIBRP (Indie Helping Indies Book Review Project) 5-star awards. *Haunted Memories*, a contemporary romance, won a contest from Ellechor Publishing House. *Against the Laws*, finaled in the Chicago-North's Fire & Ice Contest.

She loves to connect with readers. Scan Rochelle's Linktree (https://linktr.ee/rochellebradley)

where you can follow her on TikTok, Facebook, Instagram, and other social media. Visit Rochelle's website to sign up for her newsletter to keep up to date about future novels and book signings: RochelleBradley.com.

www.ingramcontent.com/pod-product-compliance
Lightning Source LLC
Chambersburg PA
CBHW030840200726
48285CB00007B/2501